# TRiM
## Saves the Day

Written by
**Deborah Hopkinson**

Illustrated by
**Kristy Caldwell**

PEACHTREE
ATLANTA

For Cheddar and his family:
Kiara, Kryn, Rye, Nile, and Cassius

—D. H.

For David, who sees everything

—K. C.

Published by
PEACHTREE PUBLISHING COMPANY INC.
1700 Chattahoochee Avenue
Atlanta, Georgia 30318-2112
*PeachtreeBooks.com*

Edited Kathy Landwehr
Design and composition by Lily Steele

The illustrations were rendered with ink, Acryla gouache, and digital tools.
Photo of Trim and Matthew Flinders, Port Lincoln, South Australia
Camloo, CC BY-SA 4.0 *https://creativecommons.org/licenses/by-sa/4.0,*
via Wikimedia Commons

Printed and bound in November 2023 at R.R. Donnelley, Dongguan, China.
10 9 8 7 6 5 4 3 2 1
First Edition
ISBN: 978-1-68263-293-2

Cataloging-in-Publication Data is available from the Library of Congress.

# Contents

# Chapter One
# Trim Wants to Help

Trim was a young ship's cat. He loved being part of the crew.

One morning, Captain Flinders called everyone together. "We have lots of jobs on our ship. Sometimes we work alone. Other times we help each other out." The captain added, "And sometimes it's all hands on deck."

"That's when we have a *really* big problem," Will told Trim.

Trim wasn't sure he wanted to see a *really* big problem. But he did want to make the captain proud. *Today I'll help all my friends*, he thought.

"What are you doing today, Penny?" Trim asked.

"I'm helping the sailors mop the deck," she said.

"I can mop too," Trim said.

Trim swished his tail. *Swish, Swish, SWISH!*
He also mewed. *Mew, Mew, MEW!*

"Trim, you're getting fur all over
the deck!" Penny cried. "Also, you're
screeching like a parrot."

A parrot? Trim knew a parrot. And he
went off to find him.

"What are you doing today, Jack?" Trim asked.

"I'm steering the ship with Captain Flinders," the parrot said.

"I can steer too," Trim said. "Watch me."
*Whee! Whee! WHEE! Mew, Mew, MEW!*

"Find your own spot, Trim," Jack screeched. "Also, screeching is *my* job."

"Then I'll help Captain Flinders decide where to go," Trim said.

## Chapter Two
# Trim Tries Harder

Trim leaped for the captain's shoulder. Just then, the ship lurched.

Trim landed on his hat instead. It's not easy to sit on a hat.

Trim dug in with his claws. He twitched his tail. *Twitch! Twitch! TWITCH! Mew, Mew, MEW!*

"Dear boy, I can't see the ocean!" Captain Flinders cried. "Also, I love when you purr, but you're mewing right in my ear."

Trim hopped down. He told Jack,
"I'll go help the gardener."

"Good idea," Jack said. "If you see any
juicy berries to eat, let me know."

The gardener was putting plants in pots.

*I can dig too*, Trim thought.

*Dig! Dig! DIG! Mew, Mew, MEW!*

"Trim, please stop! I need the dirt *inside* the pot," the gardener said. "Also, your mewing is scaring the scorpions in the nature collection."

*Scorpions are creepy and scary-looking. I wouldn't want one to get so scared it runs away,* Trim thought. *I'll go help Will.*

The ship's artist was sketching a flower.

*I can choose the right pencil,* Trim decided.

*Bat, Bat, BAT! Mew, Mew, MEW!*

"Trim, you knocked over the flower!"
Will cried. "Also, you're making a
racket."

Trim sighed. What now?

Then he remembered Cook.

*Cook is always busy,* he thought.
*He must need help in the galley.*

Cook was making biscuits in the galley.

*I can mix the dough*, Trim thought.

*Mix, Mix, MIX! Mew, Mew, MEW!*

"Trim, no paw prints in the flour, please!" Cook cried. "Also, I need quiet or I might make a mistake."

*What now?* Then Trim remembered Princess Bea. Her job was to patrol the hold to watch out for (other) rats who might eat their food.

He could definitely help Princess Bea.

## Chapter Three
# A Big Plop

The hold was dark and full of shadows. Trim saw barrels of oatmeal and flour, casks of fresh water, and crates piled with coconuts.

Trim did not see Princess Bea. *Maybe she was too tired to patrol today,* Trim thought. *I'll help her out.*

*Click! Click! CLICK!* went Trim's paws. *Mew! Mew! MEW!*

"Oh, Trim, thanks for trying to help patrol, but I finished that job," Princess Bea said. "Also, you're *so* loud. It's my naptime now."

"I give up!" Trim cried. "No one needs my help. I'll just take a bath."

Trim found himself a nice spot under a cask of water.

*All my friends are busy with their own jobs,* he thought.

Lick.

*I only wanted to help.*

Lick. Lick.

*But I haven't helped even one friend.*

Lick! Lick! LICK!

*Not even one.*

All at once, Trim felt something plop.

PLOP! Trim flicked his right ear.

PLOP! PLOP! Trim twitched his left ear.

PLOP! PLOP PLOP!

Trim shook his whole head.

He looked up.

The next plop landed right in his eye.

The plops were coming from the water cask!

25

## Chapter Four
# All Hands on Deck

"Princess Bea, wake up!" Trim yelled. "A water cask is leaking!"

"Oh no!" Princess Bea said. "That's a big problem. A *really* big problem."

Trim knew what that meant. He cried, "We need all hands on deck!"

"You're exactly right, Trim," Princess Bea said. "But how can we get everyone to come down here?"

PLOP! PLOP! PLOP! The plops were getting louder and faster.

Trim's friends hadn't needed help with their own jobs. Trim had been in the way.

He'd also made a lot of noise. But maybe now, making noise was *just* the right way to help.

"I have an idea," Trim told Princess Bea. "Better cover your ears, though."

Trim took a deep breath. He let out a tremendous yowl.

*Yowl! Yowl! YOWL!*

All over the ship, the crew stopped
what they were doing.

"That's Trim!" the captain cried.

"What a yowl! He must be in trouble," Will said.

"It sounds like he's in the hold!" Cook cried.

Trim could hear the plops getting louder.

He could also hear feet stomping, wings flapping, and paws pounding.

It was all hands and wings and paws on deck!

Trim kept on yowling.

*Yowl! Yowl! YOWL!*

"Over there, Captain!" Will cried.

"Look, Trim's head is all wet," the gardener said.

Captain Flinders said, "Shh, listen, everyone."

Plop! Plop! PLOP!

"That water cask has a leak," Cook
said. "And our little Trim has found it."

"Good job, Trim," Captain Flinders said. "You found a big problem. Now we can all work together to fix it."

"Hooray!" Jack screeched. "Trim has helped everyone!"

Trim purred happily in the captain's ear.

*Purring is a good job for me,* he thought.

*But I'm very good at yowling too.*

## Chapter Five
# The Best Ship's Cat

Cook made stew for supper.

Just as Captain Flinders speared a tasty morsel, Trim whipped it off his fork.

*Mew! Mew! MEW!* Trim asked for more. He thought the captain might say no.

Instead, the captain laughed. "Tonight, you can have as much as you want, Trim."

Cook said, "Let's raise our cups to Trim. Thanks to him, we have good, fresh water tonight."

The crew let out a great cheer. "Hip, hip, hooray! Hip, hip, hooray!"

Later that night, four friends sat under the stars.

Princess Bea said, "Thank you for helping today, Trim."

Jack bobbed his head. "Not bad for a cat."

Penny said, "Good job, Trim."

Trim felt happy. He'd helped solve a *really* big problem.

*Now I know that sometimes a ship's cat should purr,* Trim thought. *And sometimes my job is to YOWL!*

When Captain Flinders
appeared, Trim perched on
his shoulder. It was right
where he belonged.

The captain whispered, "I love you, Trim.
Someday I'll write about your adventures.
Then the whole world will know you're the
best ship's cat who ever lived."

44

And that's exactly what he did.

*TRIM SAVES THE DAY* is a made-up story about a real cat who lived in the past. We call this kind of story historical fiction.

Trim was born in 1799. Trim's owner was British explorer Matthew Flinders (1774–1814), captain of the HMS *Investigator*. As part of an expedition between 1801 and 1803, Trim became the first cat to sail around the continent of Australia.

One part of this story is not made up. Matthew Flinders tells us that Trim often ate at the captain's table. Whenever guests speared a piece of meat on their fork, but then stopped to talk, "they were often surprised to find their meat gone, they could not tell how." Trim had whipped it right off the fork!

Captain Flinders told many funny stories about his beloved cat and called him a "fearless seaman." His tribute to Trim was written in 1809 but was lost until 1971. Today there are statues of these two good friends in England and Australia. And now you know about Trim too.

Matthew Flinders wanted to explore the world because he loved reading sea adventures when he was young. I'll read this story to my cat, Beatrix. I just hope she doesn't decide to run away to sea!

What adventures will you have and write about?

# Set Sail with
# TRiM!

HC: 978-1-68263-291-8

HC: 978-1-68263-290-1

HC: 978-1-68263-293-2

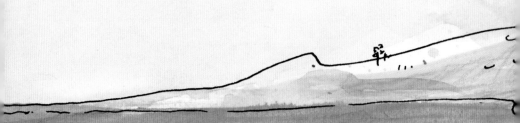